Mary
Mother of Jesus

Ellyn Sanna

Illustrated by
Ken Landgraf

BARBOUR
PUBLISHING, INC.
Uhrichsville, Ohio

© MCMXCIX by Barbour Publishing, Inc.

ISBN 1-57748-653-6

All rights reserved. No part of this publication may be reproduced or transmitted in any form or by any means without written permission of the publisher.

Some of the words spoken by the characters in this book are fiction, created by the author's imagination. Many, however, are direct quotes from the New Living Translation of the Bible (Ps. 139:1–10, 16–18, 23–24; Matt. 1:20–21, 23; 2:8, 13, 20; 3:14–17; Lk. 1:28–38, 43–55; 2:10–12, 14, 29–32, 34–35, 48–49; 3:7–11, 16, 22; Jn. 1:20–27; 2:3–10; 14:15–19, 27–28; 20:2, 17; Acts 1:7–8, 10–11).

Scripture quotations are taken from the *Holy Bible*, New Living Translation, copyright © 1996. Used by permission of Tyndale House Publishers, Inc., Wheaton, Illinois 60189, U.S.A. All rights reserved.

Published by Barbour Publishing, Inc., P.O. Box 719, Uhrichsville, Ohio 44683 http://www.barbourbooks.com

Printed in the United States of America.

Mary
Mother of Jesus

MARY RAN UP THE PATH.

1

Fifteen-year-old Mary ran up the path that led out of Nazareth, a water bucket swinging from her arm. She skimmed past the small, dusty houses, her stomach full of excited butterflies. The sun was already sinking low in the sky, and she was in a hurry to reach the well where she would draw the water for the evening meal. Joseph would be eating with her family tonight.

She had promised to marry him in a year's time, but she was still a little shy around him. Their time together was short, and they seldom had a chance to speak alone. Each time she saw him, though, she

MARY

loved him more. She hoped he felt the same about her.

Tonight she wanted to get back from the well in time to wash her face and arms, for she had been helping Ema, her mother, grind wheat all day, and she knew the fine, pale dust still clung to her skin. She did not want Joseph to see her looking grimy and sweat-streaked.

As she climbed the hill out of town, however, her feet slowed. This was her favorite time to come to the well, when most of the other women would be busy in their own homes preparing the evening meals, and Mary could walk alone, looking at the sky and the fields and the blue hills that lay along the horizon like smoke. She seldom had a chance to be by herself, but here on the empty path, with only the sound of the quiet wind murmuring through the grass, she had a chance to think and examine her heart. Here, she could open herself to God.

Long ago, when Mary was only a small child, her mother had said to her, "You have to choose, Mary. Do you want your own way? Or do you want God's way?"

SHE SELDOM HAD A CHANCE TO BE ALONE.

MARY

Mary smiled, remembering. She had been so angry that day, and she hadn't wanted Ema to start talking about God. But her mother had bent over the bread she was kneading, pressing her fingers deep into the soft dough, and then she had said, "When we accept everything that happens to us—even the things that anger us or make us sad—as gifts from God's hands, then He can use everything that happens to us for His purposes. Everything—the little things and the big things, the good things and the things that seem too hard for us to bear."

Ema's strong hands paused, and she looked up over the flat rooftop of their home. She sighed, her face troubled. "Some things are hard, even when you're grown. Look at your cousin Elizabeth who visited us last week. All her life she has prayed for a child of her own. And all this time, again and again, God tells her no. And yet Elizabeth never stops saying yes to God's will, even when she longs for something different. Even when the other women point at her and whisper because she has no children."

Ema's face cleared, and she smiled as she shaped

EMA STARTED TALKING ABOUT GOD.

MARY

the dough into a round ball. "Our God knows what is best for us. You will be surprised, Mary, how simply saying yes to God can change everything."

Mary had not understood exactly what Ema had been saying that day. Her cousin Elizabeth was much older than she was, older even than Ema, and Elizabeth's problems had not seemed as important as Mary's own. But that night when her father taught his children from the Torah and the Psalms, Mary had heard the words in a new way.

Now, as Mary reached the well, she gave a sigh of contentment, glad that no one else was there, no women gossiping about their neighbors, none of her friends giggling over the young men. For once the stone well stood empty on the high plain. Mary leaned against the windswept cedar tree, remembering again the words her father had said on that long-ago night.

"The God of Israel and the God of David is your God, too, children," Abba had told them, his deep voice gentle and full of joy. "We are His people and the sheep of His pasture. Because He is

MARY REACHED THE WELL.

MARY

your shepherd, you will always have everything that you need. You will live in the house of the Lord forever."

His words had been like a door opening wide in her heart. God was as real as Abba and Ema. . .and He loved her! The knowledge made goose bumps prick her skin.

After that, she liked to pretend that everywhere she went was God's house, each place a different room in an endless mansion. And she practiced saying yes to God every day, over and over again. Sometimes she found she could say yes to big things easier than she could to little things—but she discovered that each yes she said opened her heart that much wider to God and His love. If she said yes often enough, she reasoned, one day she would have a space inside her that would be big enough to be another room in God's great mansion. . . .

Mary glanced at the sun sinking lower in the west. She pushed the memories out of her head and leaned over the well. The cool, dark hole smelled like rain and stones, and Mary had always loved to

SHE LEANED OVER THE WELL.

MARY

peer down into its depth, looking for the blue glimmer of the sky's reflection far, far below. Today as she dropped the bucket down, she noticed her own dusty arm, and she remembered that Joseph would be at her house soon. If she didn't hurry, he would find her covered with wheat dust. She tugged the heavy load of water upward.

Murmuring a prayer of gratitude to God for the gift of clear, sweet water, she paused a moment. Despite her need to hurry, she checked to see if there were any doors in her heart she had closed in God's face, any places where she was saying no to God instead of yes. Her life was full of good gifts lately, things to which she could easily say yes—like Joseph. She smiled to herself and picked up the bucket, ready to hurry home, when a flash of light from the well stopped her. For a moment, the water in the well seemed to gleam like gold.

She bent over to peer down the dark hole, but she saw only the faint, faraway, silvery blue reflection of the evening sky. She shrugged, but as she was about to turn away, she stopped still, staring at her

A FLASH OF LIGHT STOPPED HER.

MARY

own arm. Each tiny mote of wheat dust that clung to the fine hairs on her skin glinted gold, making her arm shine as though it were reflecting fire.

Slowly, her heart pounding, she turned toward the source of the light. She sucked in a long, shaky breath and sank down with a thump on the edge of the well.

In front of her stood a tall, shining man dressed in white.

IN FRONT OF HER STOOD A TALL, SHINING MAN.

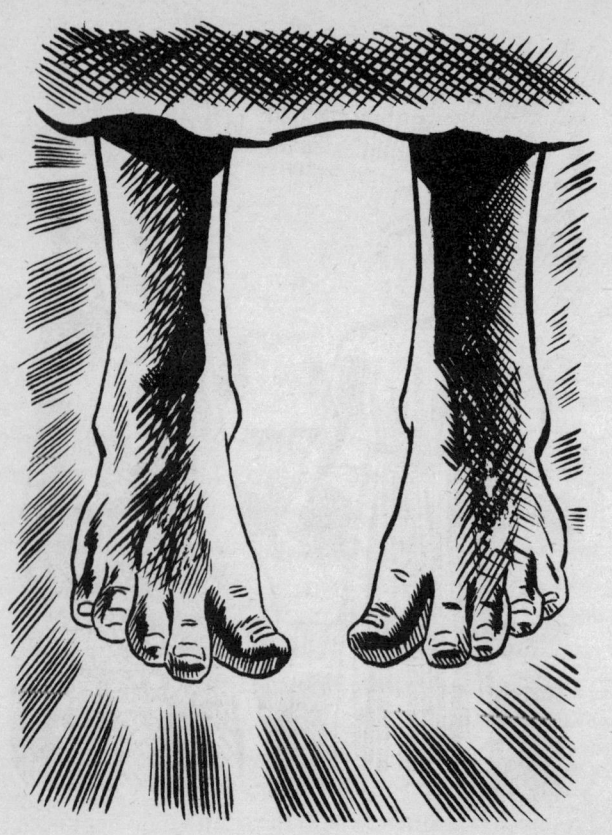

SHE STARED DOWN AT HIS FEET.

2

Light poured out of him, from his skin and clothes and face; even his hair shone, she noticed. He was in the shape of a man, but she knew he was like no man she had ever seen, and his face held something for which she could find no words. . .joy and love and strength, and something more.

Her eyes traveled from his face downward, and then her heart began to pound even harder as she stared down at his feet. They were bare, as full of light as the rest of him—and they were planted firmly in the air, a good hand's breadth above the ground. Mary slid down off the stones onto her knees,

MARY

her head bowed before this frightening creature.

"Greetings, favored woman!" the man said. "The Lord is with you!"

Mary kept her eyes fixed on the dusty ground beneath her knees. *What do you mean?* she wanted to ask. The man's words held such certainty, such joy, that she was confused. Surely he must have her confused with someone else, she thought, but when she peeked up at his face, she knew how unlikely this strange and mighty man would be to make a mistake.

"Don't be frightened, Mary," the man said.

She looked up at him. "How do you know my name?" she whispered.

The man only smiled. "God has decided to bless you!" he announced. "You will become pregnant and have a Son, and you are to name Him Jesus. He will be very great and will be called the Son of the Most High. And the Lord God will give Him the throne of His ancestor David. And He will reign over Israel forever; His Kingdom will never end!"

Mary swayed, her body trembling with terror. She put her hands flat on the ground to keep from

"GOD HAS DECIDED TO BLESS YOU!"

MARY

falling on her face and stared up at the glowing man. Desperately, she tried to pay attention to the man's words—David's throne, a prince that would be born, a kingdom that would never end.

She knew that no one had sat in David's throne for hundreds of years now, and Israel had been ruled by Rome since before she was born. . .but none of that had ever been very important to her, and she could make no sense of the man's message. She grabbed at the one thing she did understand, though, and said, "How can I become pregnant? I'm not even married yet."

The man—the creature—looked down at her for a moment, his eyes filled with a stern kindness, and then he stepped around her and sat on the edge of the well. She looked at him suspiciously, but he seemed to be resting normally on the stones, not hovering in the air as he had before. He smiled. "The Holy Spirit will come upon you, and the power of the Most High will overshadow you. So the Baby born to you will be holy, and He will be called the Son of God."

"Oh." Mary still crouched on her knees on the

"I'M NOT EVEN MARRIED YET."

MARY

ground, but the creature was much closer to her now, and she could not bear his radiance. She shut her eyes tight. How could he come from the same God whom she had loved and worshiped all her life? This was too strange, beyond anything she had ever thought about or imagined. His words frightened her.

The creature leaned back on his hands. "You know what else?" he asked, as casually as though he were one of her friends exchanging a bit of gossip. The crazy thought made her want to giggle, and she bit her lip and ducked her head, but not before she saw the creature smile, as though he had read her thoughts. "Your cousin Elizabeth is pregnant, too," he continued. "And she an old woman!"

His tone was so exactly like one used by the women who would gather at the well to discuss each other's business that a little piece of her giggle slipped out. The creature only nodded, his bright eyes shining. "People used to say Elizabeth would never have any children—but she's already in her sixth month."

Mary struggled to make sense of his words.

"ELIZABETH IS PREGNANT, TOO."

MARY

Elizabeth was having a baby. But Elizabeth was old, too old to have any children now. Ema said she had given up all hope, and now that Mary was older and understood how important babies were, she felt sorry for Elizabeth, poor wrinkled woman whose life was almost over. . . .

The creature's words made no sense. If he was a messenger from God, wouldn't God have picked a more important message to send? After all, the priests always made the Lord God seem as though He were fairly busy with men's business—and here was this strange man—this creature—this *angel* talking about babies and pregnancies: women's business. "How can this be?" she whispered.

The angel held Mary's eyes. He reached down and picked up a small stone and held it on his flat palm. Mary looked down at the stone, wondering why he had chosen an ordinary brown pebble to hold in his shining hand—and then the stone dropped straight through the angel's hand as though his flesh weren't there at all. The pebble hit the ground and bounced, and the angel laughed, a noise so full of joy

THE STONE DROPPED THROUGH THE ANGEL'S HAND.

MARY

that she caught her breath. "With God nothing is impossible."

Mary's eyes were fixed on the small, brown stone that had fallen through the creature's palm. *A magician's trick,* part of her whispered stubbornly, but when she looked back up into the angel's face, she knew that this was no magician with a bunch of sleight-of-hand tricks. No, this man, this angel, lived in the house of the Lord, just as she herself did.

A rush of understanding swept through her, and she realized that God must have many rooms in His house, rooms she had never even imagined. This bright creature had come to her from one of those other rooms she had never glimpsed.

"Will you accept this gift God has given you?" the angel asked gently.

"Now?" she whispered. "Today?"

The angel nodded.

For an instant, Mary considered what it would mean for her to become pregnant now. She pictured her parents' faces, Joseph's. . . . She gasped, feeling suddenly afraid again, but she met the angel's gaze,

"WITH GOD NOTHING IS IMPOSSIBLE."

MARY

her own eyes steady.

Love poured through her. She bowed her head, and then she spoke the word that had become so familiar to her. "Yes." She lifted her head. "May it be done to me as you have said."

Mary didn't know how long she knelt there on the damp earth beside the well. The angel had left her, she knew, but she continued to be wrapped in an awareness of God's love, a sense of His presence stronger than any she had ever experienced. She might have spent only a moment or two there with God's Spirit; she might have spent an entire lifetime.

When she came to herself, the sun was only a red line along the western horizon. Her family would be worried about her, she knew, and she picked up the bucket of water. As she hurried down the path, the water sloshing over her hand, she realized she must have been with God, outside of time, in eternity. But how was she going to explain that to Ema and Abba? How could she explain to Joseph?

SHE HURRIED DOWN THE PATH.

MARY'S HEART WAS FULL OF SHADOWS.

3

Three weeks later, early in the morning, Mary again climbed the path that led out of Nazareth, but this time she had no bucket in her hand, and she did not stop by the well. She kept on walking, deeper and deeper into the hills.

The morning sun was bright on the fields of blue flax blossoms that grew along the path, but Mary's heart was full of shadows. Her mother and father believed her now when she said she was going to have a baby, but Ema's face was lined with worry, and Abba did his work slowly, as though his arms and legs were suddenly too heavy for him to lift.

MARY

At night when the family lay on their sleeping mats, she had heard Ema and Abba whispering, talking about her until deep into the night. She caught snatches of their words: "She is a good girl, you know she. . ." "Some man. . .a stranger. . . against her will. . ." "Could it be she spoke the truth and. . .?" "This nonsense about Elizabeth having a baby, too. . ." "Mary does not lie. . . . She believes this story she told us. . ." "What will Joseph. . .?" "What shall we do?"

Each night, Mary would hear Ema's tears finally quiet, and she would hear the murmur of their prayers, and then at last their voices would be silent. But Mary would lie awake until the light of dawn came creeping through the window, her hands clasped tightly over her stomach.

During the day, she had gone about her duties quietly, tending the chickens, helping her mother make bread, caring for her younger brothers and sisters, her heart torn between joy and sorrow. She had not spoken with Joseph since that night when she had seen the angel, the night when she had told him.

MARY TENDED THE CHICKENS.

MARY

If they passed each other in the street, he turned away, his face heavy with hurt and anger. She was certain he would come to her father soon and break their betrothal, leaving her to raise God's Son alone.

Each time she reached this point in her thoughts, her heart would grow tight with fear. An unmarried woman could not give birth to a child. It was against the law. . . . But no man would want her now. Why would God ask this of her?

Climbing deeper into the hills, she said softly under her breath, "Yes, God." She drew in a deep breath and squared her shoulders. "Yes," she repeated, louder this time, though her voice wobbled a little. God would provide for both her and her Son. She would trust herself to God's care. "Yes," she said again, and now her voice was firm and sure.

Yesterday, a rumor had reached Nazareth from the hills where Elizabeth lived with her husband Zechariah: Elizabeth was expecting a child. When Ema heard the news, she had cried out, her voice full of joy and relief, and a little fear. Her eyes had flown to Mary. "You were right," she said slowly.

"YOU WERE RIGHT."

MARY

Mary nodded. "The angel told me."

"It's only a rumor," her father protested gruffly.

Last night when she lay listening to her parents' voices, she had known suddenly what she must do. The oil lamp's dim glow spilled out from the niche in the wall; Mary prayed silently in her heart while she watched the long, dark shadows flicker across the room. When her mother stepped over Mary's sleeping mat to blow out the flame, Mary caught hold of her robe.

"Ema, let me go visit Elizabeth."

Her mother crouched on the floor beside Mary. "Your father is busy with the planting now. Perhaps later, Mary."

"I want to go alone, Ema."

Her mother's hand touched her in the darkness. "It is too far for you, Mary. Especially now. . ." Her voice was troubled.

Mary sat up. "I am strong and well, Ema. And I feel the Spirit of God telling me to visit Elizabeth."

Her mother was silent for a long moment. "Very well," she said at last. "I will speak with your father."

"I WILL SPEAK WITH YOUR FATHER."

MARY

Mary had slept peacefully last night for the first time in weeks. Her parents woke her early. They ate together quietly outside in the courtyard, their voices soft so they would not wake the other children, and then they had handed her a bag packed with food and clothing. Her father reminded her of the landmarks she must follow to reach Elizabeth and Zechariah's home. Her mother had cried. As Mary told them good-bye, their faces were full of love and worry.

Mary pushed away the memory of the lines that had creased Abba's forehead and puckered Ema's mouth. She could not take away her parents' pain. And she could not foresee the future, either. She could only say yes to God one step at a time, trusting that He would take care of everything. But sometimes saying yes was so hard to do.

When her fears had pressed in on her during the past weeks, she had hoped she might see the angel again. She would have liked the comfort of his bright face, the reassurance of his joyful voice—but he had not appeared to her again, though she lingered often at the well. Sometimes she almost wondered if she

MARY TOLD THEM GOOD-BYE.

MARY

could have imagined everything that had happened. She shifted the bag over her shoulder and walked a little faster. If only Elizabeth would believe her story.

Two days later, she at last reached Zechariah and Elizabeth's small home tucked between the hills. Mary pushed her hair behind her ears and straightened her head covering. She smoothed her travel-stained robe as best she could, then took a deep breath and stuck her head inside the doorway.

"It's your cousin Mary," she called. "I've come to—"

Before she could finish, Elizabeth hurried toward her with a glad cry.

"You are favored by God above all women," she exclaimed, taking Mary's hands in hers. "Your Child will be destined for God's mightiest praise."

Mary stood silent, stunned by the joy she saw in her cousin's face. After her parents' disbelief and Joseph's rejection, Elizabeth's welcome was startling, amazing. . .and comforting. Here at last was someone who believed her, someone who would rejoice with

ELIZABETH HURRIED TOWARD HER.

MARY

her over the angel's incredible announcement.

Elizabeth tugged her gently inside the house. "Come in. Sit down and rest. You came all that way by yourself—and in your condition, too! How are you feeling? I was very, very sick the first three months—and always hungry. Let me get you something to eat."

She turned and began bustling around, bringing out a loaf of bread and a bowl of stew, a cup of water and a portion of cheese. She glanced over her shoulder at Mary and chuckled. "You looked so shocked for a moment there when I flew at you before you could barely get a word out. Zechariah's always telling me to calm down. But this. . ." She patted her large, round belly, then waved her hand at Mary. "It's all so exciting. So amazing. I can't calm down."

She set the food in front of Mary, then sat down beside her. Her voice was soft now as she said, "I am honored that the mother of my Lord should visit me."

Mary looked at her cousin. Her hair was as white as ever, and her face was still lined, but her

"COME IN. SIT DOWN AND REST."

MARY

cheeks were as flushed as a child's, and her eyes shone. "How did you know?" Mary asked her, though anything seemed possible to her now.

Elizabeth smiled and patted her stomach again. "When you came in and greeted me, the instant I heard your voice, my baby moved in me for joy!" She leaned over and touched Mary's hand. "Go on now, child. You need to eat. The miracle inside you is flesh and blood, remember. You'd better feed the both of you!"

While Mary ate, Elizabeth told her own story, about the angel who had come to Zechariah. Zechariah had lost his voice because he hadn't believed the angel's news, and now he could only communicate through writing. Fascinated, Mary listened silently, but then Elizabeth wanted to know Mary's story, too. Mary took a last bite of stew, and then, shyly at first, she told Elizabeth everything that had happened. The more she told, the faster the words tumbled out of her mouth. She was so relieved to have someone who finally understood!

When she had finished, Elizabeth sat back and

MARY TOLD ELIZABETH EVERYTHING THAT HAD HAPPENED.

MARY

smiled. For a long moment, she was silent, her lips moving, and Mary knew she was praying. Then Elizabeth's smile grew wider, and she said, "You have always given your whole heart to God. You have believed that He would do what He said. That is why He has given you this wonderful blessing."

Suddenly, Mary felt as though joy was blossoming inside her, spreading wider and wider until she could no longer contain it. She burst out, "Oh, how I praise the Lord. How I rejoice in God my Savior! For He took notice of His lowly servant girl, and now generation after generation will call me blessed. For He, the Mighty One, is holy, and He has done great things for me. His mercy goes on from generation to generation, to all who fear Him. His mighty arm does tremendous things!

"How He scatters the proud and haughty ones! He has taken princes from their thrones and exalted the lowly. He has satisfied the hungry with good things and sent the rich away with empty hands.

"And how He has helped His servant Israel! He has not forgotten His promise to be merciful. For He

"YOU HAVE ALWAYS GIVEN YOUR WHOLE HEART TO GOD."

MARY

promised our ancestors—Abraham and his children—to be merciful to them forever."

Mary understood now why she had felt God's Spirit telling her to visit Elizabeth. Surrounded by Elizabeth's delighted love and understanding, Mary could begin to prepare for the Savior's birth. She leaned back in her chair, her hands pressed against her belly, and her heart spilled over with awe and joy.

Her weeks with Elizabeth passed quickly. The age difference between them no longer seemed to matter, and the two women spent long hours talking about pregnancy and God, babies and miracles. Some evenings as they sat around the supper table, they laughed until they cried, while Zechariah listened and chuckled silently. Other evenings, they sat up on the rooftop, gazing up at the stars that sprinkled the deep blue sky, praying softly together. Mary watched Elizabeth's round stomach swell larger and larger, and all the while she delighted in the growing changes in her own body.

At last, after three months, Elizabeth decided

ZECHARIAH CHUCKLED SILENTLY.

MARY

that it was time Mary returned to Nazareth, before traveling became any more difficult for her. Mary was disappointed not to stay for the birth of Elizabeth's baby. He was due any day now, but she knew Elizabeth was right. Besides, it was time she once again faced her parents. . .and Joseph.

As they said good-bye, Elizabeth and Mary clung to each other and cried. "I will be praying for you," Elizabeth whispered. "Don't be afraid. God will work everything out."

Zechariah pressed Mary's hand silently. And then she squared her shoulders and turned toward the path that would lead her over the hills to Nazareth. By now, she thought as she walked, Joseph would surely have asked her father to release him from their betrothal. But God would be with her. . .no matter what.

The journey home passed quickly. She sang psalms as she walked, and at night she felt God's presence all around her as she slept. He was her companion wherever she went. Over and over, she hummed the

AT NIGHT SHE FELT GOD'S PRESENCE.

MARY

words of her favorite psalm:

*O Lord, you have examined my heart
and know everything about me.
You know when I sit down or stand up.
You know my every thought when far away.
You chart the path ahead of me
and tell me where to stop and rest.
Every moment you know where I am.
You know what I am going to say even before
    I say it, Lord.
You both precede and follow me.
You place your hand of blessing on my head.
Such knowledge is too wonderful for me,
    too great for me to know!
I can never escape from your spirit!
I can never get away from your presence!
If I go up to heaven, you are there;
If I go down to the place of the dead,
    you are there.
If I ride the wings of the morning,
if I dwell by the farthest oceans,*

EVERY MOMENT YOU KNOW WHERE I AM.

MARY

even there your hand will guide me,
and your strength will support me.
You saw me before I was born.
Every day of my life was recorded in your book.
Every moment was laid out
before a single day had passed.
How precious are your thoughts about me,
    O God!
They are innumerable!
I can't even count them;
they outnumber the grains of sand!
And when I wake up in the morning,
you are still with me!
Search me, O God, and know my heart;
test me and know my thoughts.
Point out anything in me that offends you,
and lead me along the path of everlasting life.

As she sang, Mary was filled with a joy like she had never imagined was possible.

But as she drew closer to Nazareth, her feet moved slower. At last she stood on the hill above the

SHE STOOD ON THE HILL.

MARY

village and looked down at the familiar houses. From here, their flat roofs and square clay walls made them look like a set of children's blocks scattered in the dusty valley. Mary drew in a deep breath and started down the hill. "I want Your will, Lord," she whispered. "Whatever it is. . . ."

As she entered the narrow streets, her feet automatically started to take her to the small lane where Joseph's carpentry shop was. For the last couple of years, she had always snatched at any excuse to walk past his shop, hoping to catch a glimpse of him bent over his work or—better yet—exchange smiles and shy greetings with him. This time, though, she hesitated. Everything was different now.

Still, she had nothing of which to be ashamed. If he had decided to reject her, that was his right; she would grieve for him, but she would not hang her head. Not when the Son of God had already begun to flutter and kick inside her. "Yes," she said softly. "Whatever You want, Father."

She lifted her chin and started down the lane.

SHE ENTERED THE NARROW STREETS.

"I'VE MISSED YOU, MARY."

4

Before she had taken more than a few steps, she found her shoulders grabbed from behind. She jumped and twirled around.

"It *is* you." Joseph stood looking down at her, breathing heavily as though he had been running. "You're home. I was just coming from your parents' when I thought I saw you up ahead. . ." He drew in a deep breath while she stared at him with surprise; it almost sounded as though his voice was full of welcome. . .and something else that sounded like relief. She frowned, puzzled.

"I've missed you, Mary," he said softly, his hand

MARY

still warm on her shoulder. "I was afraid you would never come home." And then he drew her closer, and his arms went tight around her. Mary let out a long trembly breath and pressed her face against his robe's rough fabric.

At last they stepped away from each other and smiled shyly. Mary searched his face. "You believe me now?"

He nodded. "Forgive me for not believing what you told me right from the beginning. But I. . ." He shrugged. His face clouded.

Mary touched his troubled mouth with her hand, delighted by her own daring. "It's all right," she said softly. "I understand. What changed your mind?"

He pressed his lips against her fingers, then took her hand and began walking with her.

"I have to be honest with you," he said, and she heard the shame and regret in his voice. "I had decided to break our betrothal. I did not want you to be publicly disgraced, so I was going to do it quietly. But I was dreading talking to your father." He gave her a quick sideways glance. "And I hated to think I

"I HAVE TO BE HONEST WITH YOU."

MARY

wasn't going to spend the rest of my life with you after all."

He touched a strand of her hair that had escaped her head covering. "One night as I was trying to think what I should do—and how I should do it—my thoughts kept circling round and round. I thought I would never fall asleep. I tried to pray, to put the end of our betrothal in God's hands, but I could find no peace.

"At last I must have fallen asleep. My dreams were broken, bits and pieces of nightmares. And then suddenly I realized that a. . .a being was standing next to my bed. The being was dressed in white, and he glowed so bright that my dark room was as light as noonday. At first I was frightened, but when I looked into the being's face, I saw he was smiling. . ." His voice trailed away, as though he were still overwhelmed with wonder.

Mary nodded eagerly. "His name is Gabriel. That's what he told Zechariah."

Joseph stopped walking and turned to face her. "So your cousin's husband saw an angel, too? And

"A BEING WAS STANDING NEXT TO MY BED."

MARY

you. . .and me. . ." His eyes met hers. "These are amazing times, Mary. To think that God is doing this. . .unbelievable thing in our life. *Our* Child. . ." He fell silent, his eyes bright with awe.

"What did the angel say?" Mary prompted quietly.

Joseph drew in a deep sigh and began walking again. "I remember word by word—I've thought about it so many times while I waited for you to come home. He said, 'Joseph, son of David, do not be afraid to go ahead with your marriage to Mary. For the Child within her has been conceived by the Holy Spirit. And she will have a Son, and you are to name Him Jesus, for He will save His people from their sins.'"

Joseph stopped walking and faced Mary again, his face blazing with excitement. "Remember, Mary, what the prophet Isaiah said—'The virgin will conceive a child! She will give birth to a Son, and He will be called Immanuel.'"

Joseph's eyes dropped to Mary's stomach. "Think about what those names mean, Mary," he said softly.

"YOU ARE TO NAME HIM JESUS."

MARY

"Jesus means 'the Lord saves.' And Immanuel—'God is with us.' " His voice shook with wonder.

The Baby fluttered inside Mary's stomach, and she felt goose bumps run up her arms. "Yes," she whispered. "Yes."

Joseph looked into her eyes. "Will you marry me, Mary? Now? Tomorrow? As soon as we can?"

She smiled at the eagerness in his voice. "Yes," she said again.

Now that Joseph had also seen the angel, her parents believed her at last. With relief and joy and awe they gave Mary to Joseph in marriage. Ema and Mary's sisters helped her pack her linens and other belongings, and Abba and her brothers carried them to Joseph's small house nearby. The days after her wedding were happy ones.

But just as she was settling down to wait for the birth of her Son, Joseph came home one afternoon from his carpenter's shop, his face troubled.

"What is it?" Mary asked him after he had washed his hands and said a prayer of thanksgiving for their

"WILL YOU MARRY ME, MARY?"

MARY

supper. "What's worrying you?"

Joseph took a swallow of the lentil soup Mary had made. Then he sighed. "It's that emperor in Rome. He's decided he wants a census taken of the entire nation. Everyone has to go to the city of their ancestors." He met Mary's eyes. "I'm sorry. I hate to have you traveling now. We're going to have to go to Bethlehem."

"WE'RE GOING TO HAVE TO GO TO BETHLEHEM."

SHE LOOKED AROUND BETHLEHEM'S BUSY STREETS.

5

This wasn't what Mary had expected. As she looked around Bethlehem's busy streets, her heart longed for home. She missed quiet Nazareth; she missed her mother's gentle hands and her father's smile. She had imagined her baby being born at home, where she would have felt safe and loved. Not here in this strange, bustling place, full of the noise of animals and the frustrated voices of too many people in too small a space.

Joseph hadn't even been able to find them a room in the inn. Mary sighed and leaned over their donkey's back as Joseph led it to the stable behind

MARY

the inn. At least she could get down soon, and then surely there would be somewhere she could lie down....

Once she was stretched out on Joseph's cloak on top a pile of straw, she fell asleep almost immediately. She didn't sleep long, though. When she opened her eyes, she looked around the stable. Their donkey was eating hay next to a tired-looking cow, and two sleepy chickens roosted on the rafter above her head. A sheep lay in the straw beside Mary, its legs tucked neatly beneath it while it thoughtfully chewed its cud.

Mary pushed herself up and rubbed her back, then settled back against the manger. The air was filled with the smell of animals, but at least it was quiet and peaceful here. *Yes, Lord,* she prayed. *Even here, even now. If this is where You want Your Son to be born, then I will still say yes.*

Joseph came through the stable door, carrying the supper he had bought them at the inn. His eyes were worried as he looked down at Mary. "How are you? Can you eat anything?"

MARY LOOKED AROUND THE STABLE.

MARY

She shook her head. Joseph knelt beside her, his hands on her shoulders. He met her eyes. "How soon do you think it will be until. . . ?"

Mary took a shaky breath and smiled. "Soon."

Later that night, tears of joy streaked her face as she looked down at her newborn Son. She touched His tiny, squirming feet, and ran a finger along His petal-soft cheek. Then carefully, as she had seen Ema do with her younger brothers and sisters, she wrapped Him tight and warm in clean swaddling cloths. Exhausted, she drifted off to sleep, holding in her arms God in a tiny human body.

An hour or two later, Joseph shook her gently awake. "We have visitors," he told her softly.

Mary reached for the Baby, but her lap was empty. Joseph must have laid Him in the manger; He was still sleeping soundly, undisturbed. She looked up and found the stable door crowded with strange men. She wiped the sleep from her eyes and sat up. They were shepherds, she realized, for some of them still clutched their shepherds' crooks in their gnarled

SHE WRAPPED HIM IN SWADDLING CLOTHS.

MARY

hands. Their eyes were wide with wonder.

"We were w–w–watching our sheep," one of them stuttered, "w–when all of a sudden a strange man was there w–with us on the hill. We—"

"He shone so bright that it might as well have been midday," another interrupted. "We were scared, but—"

"He told us not to be afraid," the first one finished.

A younger man stepped into the doorway. He was barely more than a boy, Mary saw, and his bright gaze was fastened on the Baby where He lay in the manger. "The angel said to us, 'Don't be afraid! I bring you good news of great joy for everyone! The Savior—yes, the Messiah, the Lord—has been born tonight in Bethlehem, the city of David!'" The boy's eyes were dreamy as he quoted the angel's words. "He told us that we would recognize the Baby because He would be like this—" He waved a hand at the Baby. "Lying in a manger, wrapped tight in strips of cloth." The boy's eyes were full of stars as he turned back to Mary. "And then suddenly the angel was joined by more angels, hundreds and

"THE MESSIAH HAS BEEN BORN IN BETHLEHEM."

MARY

hundreds of them filling up the sky. They were singing."

"Did you understand their song?" Mary asked softly, curious to know more about these heavenly creatures.

The shepherd boy nodded. "They sang, 'Glory to God in the highest heaven, and peace on earth, goodwill among people.'" He sighed and fell silent.

"And then we left our sheep and ran all the way here," the first shepherd said. He added gruffly, "We wanted to see for ourselves."

Mary smiled at the shepherds, and then she leaned over the manger. Gently, she unwrapped the Baby a little so they could see His face. Joseph motioned for the shepherds to come into the stable, and they filed in, then stood in a cluster looking down at the Baby. He squirmed, then opened His eyes and looked gravely up toward the shepherds' hovering faces. After a moment, one by one, the shepherds went down on their knees.

When they had gone, Mary leaned against Joseph's

THE SHEPHERDS WENT DOWN ON THEIR KNEES.

MARY

shoulder, thinking over everything that had happened. The Baby slept peacefully in Joseph's arms now, and even the cow and the sheep had fallen asleep. The whole world was hushed and quiet. *If my heart is Your mansion, Lord,* Mary thought sleepily, *then how full the rooms are getting with treasures.*

She let her eyes fall shut, glad that she had dared to say yes to God. As she drifted off to sleep, her last thought was, *What wonderful thing will You do next, God?*

THE BABY SLEPT PEACEFULLY.

MARY HELD JESUS IN HER ARMS.

6

Eight days later, Mary and Joseph took the Baby to be circumcised in the synagogue. At the ceremony, they gave Him the name the angel had told Joseph to use: Jesus. It was a common name in Galilee; no one raised an eyebrow when they told the rabbi the name they had chosen for their Son.

But Mary and Joseph looked at each other and smiled. They knew that their Baby's name had not been chosen by them. It had been given to them by the angel Gabriel, and its meaning would be fulfilled by their Child's life. *The Lord saves.* Mary said the words to herself as she held Jesus in her arms. Every

MARY

time she said her Child's name, she realized, she would be affirming her faith in God. *The Lord saves!*

A month or so later, the time came for Mary and Joseph to go to the temple in Jerusalem. Jewish law said that on the fortieth day after a son's birth the mother must go to the temple to be purified. The Torah also said, "If a woman's first child is a boy, he must be dedicated to the Lord." So Mary carefully packed their clothes for the short trip, tucking plenty of diapers for Jesus into their bags.

When they reached Jerusalem, they made their way through the busy streets to the temple. Joseph carried a cage with two pigeons for a sacrifice to God. Mary carried Jesus in her arms. She held Him carefully, fearful that the crowd might jostle Him out of her arms, her cheek pressed against His soft head.

As soon as she had said yes to the angel's message, she had begun to love Him, and she had learned to love Him more during the months when she had carried Him inside her body. But now that He was here, where she could hold Him in her arms, look into His eyes, and touch His tiny hands, she loved

JOSEPH CARRIED A CAGE WITH TWO PIGEONS.

MARY

Him in a new and different way. He was hers...her Baby. Her heart nearly broke every time she thought of danger threatening Him. She would do anything to keep Him safe.

As they neared the temple, Mary looked up at the tall columns, and she held Jesus even tighter. For some reason, she was dreading today's ceremony. Something inside her didn't want to give Jesus to God. He was hers. She sighed and followed Joseph through the bronze gate that led into the women's court of the temple.

Before they could go very far, an old man came up to them, his face bright with welcome and joy. He almost seemed to have been waiting for them, Mary thought, and yet she was certain she had never seen him before.

"My name is Simeon," he said, and his old voice quavered with emotion, as though he might cry. His eyes were fixed on the bundle in Mary's arms. "May I see your Child?"

Mary hesitated, but something in the man's old, wrinkled face reassured her. She unwrapped

"MY NAME IS SIMEON."

MARY

Jesus' covering and turned Him so that the old man could see His face.

Simeon let out a long sigh. "At last," he breathed. "At last." He shut his eyes, and his lips moved silently in prayer. After a moment, he smiled and opened his eyes. "I have been waiting for this moment for a long, long time."

Joseph was studying the old man's face thoughtfully. "What do you mean?" he asked.

Simeon turned to Joseph. "I am an old man." His smile grew wider. "As you can no doubt see. Over the years, I have watched our nation fall deeper and deeper under Rome's control, and I have grieved for Israel. I am all alone, for my wife and my sons and daughters have all died. Year after year, I grew more and more lonely—but still I continued to pray to God to rescue our nation. I believed that the Messiah would come, just as the prophets said He would. But year after year, nothing changed. I saw no sign of the Messiah. And I grew lonelier and lonelier.

"Some years ago, I told God that I was ready to die and be with Him. But I felt God's Spirit tell me,

"I HAVE BEEN WAITING FOR THIS MOMENT."

MARY

'No. This is not your time.' After that I was filled with a strange restlessness. I continued to pray—and one day I felt the Spirit say to me, as clear as I hear you, 'You will not die until you see the Lord's Messiah.' "

Simeon turned away from Joseph, back to Jesus, his faded eyes bright with tears. "This morning I was enjoying the sunshine in my garden, when I felt the Spirit nudge me. 'Get up,' it said to me. 'Go to the temple.' " Simeon shrugged. "At first I told myself it was my imagination. But then the Spirit's call was too clear to be mistaken. And so I came. . .and as I walked through the gate, I saw the Baby."

His lined face was soft with love. "Could I hold Him, do you think?" He turned toward Mary, his voice humble. "Just for a moment?"

Mary smiled and held Jesus out to him. Simeon took the Baby in his arms, and for a long moment he looked down into Jesus' face. The Baby looked back at him soberly, then reached out and tangled His small fist in Simeon's long, white beard. Simeon smiled.

SIMEON SMILED.

MARY

"Lord," he said softly, his voice full of adoration and awe, "now I can die in peace! As You promised me, I have seen the Savior You have given to all people. He is a light to reveal God to the nations, and He is the glory of Your people Israel!"

Joseph and Mary exchanged looks of surprise. They knew their Son was special; they had not forgotten all the angels who had been involved with His coming. And yet now that He was here and they were so busy caring for Him, feeding Him, and changing His diapers, sometimes they forgot that He was not only *their* Baby, but the Savior.

Simeon looked into Mary's face. "This Baby belongs to all of us," he said gently, and she heard the understanding in his voice. "God sent Him for us all."

He put the Baby back in her arms, and then he raised his hands and blessed both her and Joseph. When he had finished praying, he again turned to Mary. His eyes met hers for a long moment.

"This Child will be rejected by many in Israel," he said, "and it will be their undoing. But He will be the greatest joy to many others. The deepest thoughts

"THIS BABY BELONGS TO ALL OF US."

MARY

of many hearts will be revealed." Simeon's face was grave, and he reached out and touched Mary's hand where it clasped Jesus. "And a sword will pierce your very soul, Daughter."

Mary felt a shiver run across her skin. "What do you—?" she started to ask, but before she could finish her question, an old woman rushed up to her, her wrinkled face glowing with joy.

"Praise God!" the woman cried. She looked at Jesus, and tears of joy ran down her lined cheeks. "Praise God! He is here at last!"

Simeon nodded. "Yes, Anna, He is here at last."

The two old people spent a long time with Mary and Joseph and the Baby. They put their gnarled fingers in His tiny hands, they smiled down into His face, they took turns holding Him close against their hearts. Mary smiled as she watched them, but inside her heart, she was hearing again Simeon's words: *A sword will pierce your very soul.*

But Jesus' birth had brought her nothing but joy. How could anything about Him ever send a sword into her soul?

"PRAISE GOD! HE IS HERE AT LAST!"

MARY

As they said good-bye to Simeon and Anna, she pushed the thought away. Surely, Simeon was wrong. He was so old after all.

As they crossed the temple courtyard to give their pigeons to the priest, she looked back over her shoulder at Simeon and Anna. Anna was praising God again, her cracked old voice loud with triumph. Everyone who passed by her she grabbed and cried, "Have you heard what has happened?" Mary could hear her from all the way across the courtyard. But Simeon was still standing where they had left him, watching them. Across the courtyard, his eyes met Mary's.

The compassion in his gaze made her hold Jesus tighter. *He knows what lies ahead,* she realized. *God's Spirit has told him.* She looked down at Jesus' small, downy head, and her eyes burned with tears.

But the time had come now for them to give Jesus to God. Mary turned Jesus around in her arms, but before she handed Him to the priest, she hesitated for a long moment. She looked down into her

MARY HESITATED FOR A LONG MOMENT.

MARY

Son's face. *How can I bear it if something should ever happen to Him?*

Joseph touched her arm. "Mary?"

She sighed. A tear rolled down her cheek. *Yes, Lord,* her heart whispered. *Even then, if You should allow something to happen to this precious One... even then, I still say yes. He is Yours. You gave Him to me. Now I give Him back to You.* She put her Baby in the priest's arms to be dedicated to God.

Mary and Joseph took the Baby back to the house they had rented in Bethlehem. Joseph had opened a small carpentry shop to support them, and Mary was busy caring for the Baby. Each day He seemed to grow bigger, and they were delighted by all the new things He was learning to do. He could sit up; then He could crawl; then He could pull Himself up on His tottery, plump legs.

"E-ma!" He called early one morning, waking them from their sleep, and together they celebrated His first word. The next week He learned to say *Abba*, and then He was stringing whole chains of

JOSEPH OPENED A SMALL CARPENTRY SHOP.

MARY

words together, babbling at Mary while she ground their grain, playing at Joseph's feet with scraps of wood, chuckling to Himself. Each day, they loved Him more.

And then one evening, when Jesus was nearly two years old, three strangers came to their door.

MARY GROUND THEIR GRAIN.

A MAN IN A LONG SILK ROBE STOOD IN THE DOORWAY.

7

"We have company, Mary," Joseph said as he came in from his shop.

He hadn't had a chance to wash yet, she saw when she looked up from her sewing, for he had sawdust clinging to his beard and hair. She smiled and looked past him, expecting to see one of the neighbors from down the street. Instead, a man in a long silk robe stood in the doorway. Startled, Mary put down her sewing and got to her feet.

The man's eyes were different than any she had ever seen, and his skin was another shade of tan than their own. He held his head proudly, but his eyes

MARY

were full of curiosity and wonder.

"Come in," Joseph said to him and motioned him deeper into their house. The man's long robe whispered on the dirt floor as he came toward Mary—and behind him followed two more men, each dressed as richly as he. Their narrow faces were full of wisdom and pride.

Jesus had been playing quietly in the corner with the wooden blocks Joseph had made Him, but now He toddled forward to investigate these newcomers. When they saw Him, the three men's faces changed. Mary was suddenly reminded of the way the shepherds' faces had looked on the night when Jesus was born—awed and humbled and joyful, all at the same time. *They know*, she realized. *These men know who my Son is.*

Amazed, she watched as the three proud men in their rich robes went down on their knees on her dirt floor. They bowed their heads before her little Son. Mary turned toward Jesus, wondering what He would do. He stood still for a moment, looking gravely at the three men—and then He smiled and

THE THREE PROUD MEN KNELT.

MARY

came forward. One by one, He gently put His small hands on their faces. Mary and Joseph watched while tears leaked out of the men's eyes and ran down their proud cheeks.

"We are royal astrologers," one of the three men explained over dinner. "We come from a land far to the East. Almost two years ago, we saw a new star in the East, and we knew that the time had come for the King of the Jews to be born. We wanted to worship Him, and so we followed the star." He paused and looked across the table at Jesus. "The star brought us here."

"But we stopped first to ask directions from Herod," one of the others reminded.

"Herod?" Joseph frowned.

"We went to Jerusalem first," explained the third man. "We were expecting to find the new king among the royal court." His eyes traveled around the small room, and then his gaze settled on Jesus' face. "We should have known better," he murmured.

"What did Herod have to say?" Joseph asked

"WHAT DID HEROD SAY?"

MARY

uneasily. He didn't trust Herod, Mary knew, especially not since they had heard of the murders in Herod's own house. Herod had killed his own family to ensure his rule—and meanwhile he strictly followed the Torah's diet, never eating any pork or other meat that the Law did not allow. "As though that will do him any good when he stands before God," Joseph would mutter. "The hypocrite. I'd rather be Herod's pig than Herod's son."

Thinking of Herod made Mary shiver. She wanted to scoop Jesus up on her lap and hold Him tight, but He was eating happily, sharing bites of food with the astrologer beside Him.

"What did Herod say?" Joseph repeated.

The three men exchanged glances. "He was upset," one of them admitted. "Obviously, he knew of no ruler but himself—and he wasn't happy about the idea. He called a meeting of all the priests and rabbis, and he asked them where your prophets had predicted that the Messiah would be born. They were the ones who first directed us toward Bethlehem."

Another of the men stroked his long black beard

THE THREE MEN EXCHANGED GLANCES.

MARY

thoughtfully. "After that, Herod sent for us privately. He spent a long time asking us questions about the star we had seen."

"What sort of questions?" Joseph asked, his voice tense.

"He wanted to know exactly when we had first seen the star."

Mary looked from Joseph's worried face to Jesus' unconcerned one. *Herod knows about our Son now,* she realized. *And he knows about how old He is.* Fear clutched at her, but then Jesus smiled at His mother. Her heart lightened, and she smiled back at Him before turning once more to the three astrologers. "Did Herod say anything else?" she asked.

Again the three men glanced at each other. "He told us to go to Bethlehem and search carefully for the Child," one of them said.

" 'And when you find Him,' " one of the other astrologers mimicked Herod's gruff voice, " 'come back and tell me so that I can go and worship Him, too!' "

Across the table, Mary and Joseph met each other's eyes.

"HEROD TOLD US TO SEARCH FOR THE CHILD."

MARY

When they had finished eating, the astrologers brought in their packs from their camels. They opened them and brought out treasure chests full of gold and frankincense. "These are for the Child," one of them said.

Jesus explored the costly gifts with His small chubby hands, delighted by the bright colors of the jewels that studded the chests. When He found a brilliant blue and scarlet feather tucked in among the gold, He was more pleased with that than with anything else. Even Joseph, who had barely spoken since supper, laughed as he watched Him play.

Amid the commotion, Mary watched her husband's face. He was uncomfortable and awed by the riches spilled out across his floor, she knew, but the tension in his face was caused by something more than embarrassment. He was worried about Herod.

One of the astrologers placed yet another gift at Jesus' feet. "My gift," he said quietly. "Myrrh."

Mary shivered, and her eyes sought Joseph's. He gave a little shrug of his shoulders, as though he were

THE ASTROLOGERS BROUGHT IN THEIR PACKS.

MARY

advising her not to make too much of the astrologer's strange gift. After all, perhaps in their country they did not use myrrh as a spice for burial. Still, it seemed like an odd gift for a Baby. She reached for Jesus and held Him close. His little body was warm and wiggly against her, and she refused to think that anyone would ever wrap His dead body with white linen and myrrh. Surely, God would keep His Son safe from death. He of all people would never have to face death's cold darkness.

The three astrologers spent the night outside the house, sleeping on the ground with their camels, and in the morning they came inside again to eat with Mary and Joseph and Jesus. Mary was tired, for her sleep had been broken, but she tried to smile as she handed out the food bowls. "Did you sleep well?"

"No," the oldest one said. "We did not." He looked at the others, as though he wondered what more he should say.

"Our sleep was troubled by dreams," another of them said.

THEY SPENT THE NIGHT OUTSIDE.

MARY

The one whose skin was darker than the others met Mary's eyes. "We will be on our way this morning, back to our own land. But we will not go through Jerusalem this time. We will not return to Herod as he requested."

Mary heard Joseph let out a long breath. "Why not?" he asked gruffly.

The dark-skinned astrologer turned toward him. "God spoke to me," he said simply. "In a dream. He told me not to tell Herod what we found here." His eyes went to Jesus. Jesus looked back at him and smiled. "We will not tell him," the man said softly.

The astrologers spent the morning with Jesus, quietly watching Him play and listening to His voice, and then they went on their way. After they were gone, Joseph went back to his shop. He had said very little all morning, and Mary could see the lines of tension that creased his forehead. She held Jesus on her lap for a long time, rocking Him and singing to Him, her heart full of fears for the future.

"Mary! Wake up, Mary!"

"GOD SPOKE TO ME."

MARY

In the middle of the night, Joseph's voice made her jump up from her sleep, her heart pounding. She stared around the dark house. "What is it?"

"I had a dream." Joseph's voice was soft and urgent. "I saw the angel again. We have to leave."

"Now?" Mary's heart was heavy with dread. She scrambled across their sleeping mat and touched Jesus' tousled curls where He lay sleeping quietly beside them. "What did—what did the angel say?" she whispered.

Joseph took a deep breath. "He said, 'Get up and flee to Egypt with the Child and His mother. Stay there until I tell you to return, because Herod is going to try to kill the Child.' "

Mary sank back on their mat, her hand still resting on Jesus' head. "Can we wait until morning?" She hated to wake Jesus. She hated to set out with Him in the darkness for a strange land where she had never been. "Why Egypt?"

Joseph had already lit a lamp and was starting to pack their belongings. "Come on, Mary," he said over his shoulder. "We may not have much time.

"WE MAY NOT HAVE MUCH TIME."

MARY

Herod may already be sending his soldiers to search out all the baby boys."

Mary hesitated a moment longer. They were settled here in Bethlehem now. They had been so happy these last two years. She closed her eyes tightly. "Yes, Lord," she whispered at last. "I will accept whatever You want."

She got to her feet and began to pack for the long journey to Egypt.

MARY BEGAN TO PACK FOR THE LONG JOURNEY.

JESUS WAS ALSO AWAKE.

8

Almost a year later, Mary lay watching the morning sun shine through the window of their small Egyptian house. Jesus was also awake, but although He turned His head now and then to smile at His mother, He, too, was silent, lying quietly as He watched the sunlight filter through the palm fronds beyond the window.

Beside her, Joseph was still asleep. All night, he had tossed and turned, muttering in his sleep, and Mary hated to wake him, though she knew he would need to leave soon for his carpentry shop. She should get up and stir the fire to life, dress herself

MARY

and Jesus, and prepare their morning meal. And after that, she should go to the market to buy food for their supper.

She sighed. Life seemed so much more complicated here in Egypt where everyone spoke a different language, where her family and friends were so far away. A simple thing like going to the market wore her out. For just a moment longer, she decided, she would simply lie here, enjoying the morning quiet, close to the two people she loved most in all the world.

"Would you like to start home today?" asked Joseph's quiet voice.

Her heart leaped. She turned her head and saw that Joseph's eyes were open.

He nodded, answering the unspoken question in her eyes. "I saw the angel again last night. He said, 'Get up and take the Child and His mother back to the land of Israel, because those who were trying to kill the Child are dead.' " Joseph ran his thumb gently along Mary's cheek. "We can go home now, Mary. He'll be safe."

LIFE SEEMED SO MUCH MORE COMPLICATED IN EGYPT.

MARY

Tears of joy stung Mary's eyes. She closed her eyes and whispered a prayer of praise to God.

The trip home was a happy one, not like the rushed and fearful journey the year before when they had fled from Herod. This time they laughed and talked and enjoyed the scenery. Jesus was old enough that they could point things out to Him, and He looked at everything with interest and delight.

As they traveled closer to Bethlehem, the hills began to look familiar, and Mary grew excited at the thought of being back with her friends. They reached Judea late one afternoon, and Mary told Jesus, "Maybe we'll sleep tonight in Bethlehem, where You were born."

They stopped to rest for a moment beside the road. While Mary gave Jesus a drink and a bite of bread, Joseph heard the noise of travelers coming toward them. "Let me go hear what news they have of Bethlehem," he said and walked down the road to meet them.

He stood talking with the travelers for a long

THE TRIP HOME WAS A HAPPY ONE.

MARY

time before they went on their way. When he turned back toward her, Mary's heart sank at the stern look on his face. "I don't like it," he said to her when he had rejoined his family. "Herod's will left Judea to his son Archelaus. They say he hates the Jews even more than his father did. He has already put to death hundreds of our people."

Mary reached for Jesus' small hand and clutched it tightly. He looked up at her, His little face full of love and peace, and she smiled down at Him. "It will be all right," she told Joseph. "The angel would not have told you to come home if we would not be safe."

Joseph nodded, but his eyes were still clouded with worry. "We will spend the night here," he said at last, "instead of pressing on for Bethlehem. I will pray about this. I want to be sure we are doing what God wants."

Mary nodded. "I will pray, too." She thought of Gabriel, the angel who had spoken to her nearly four years before. Although she had never seen him again, she believed he was the same angel who spoke to

HE LOOKED UP AT HER.

MARY

Joseph in his dreams. She liked to think of him walking with them each day, invisible to their eyes, his bright face turned always toward her Son, making sure no harm befell Him. Heaven was watching over Jesus, she had no doubt, and she smiled at Joseph, trying to reassure him. "God will take care of us," she told him as they began to make camp for the night. "We don't need to be afraid."

When Mary awoke the next morning, Joseph was already up, getting their donkey ready for the day's journey. Jesus was helping him, chattering to His father all the while. Mary smiled and stretched, then got up and prepared their morning meal.

Once they had eaten, they lifted Jesus on the donkey and began to walk. Joseph was not leading them toward Bethlehem, though, Mary realized. She looked up at him, surprised. "Where are we going?"

"What would you think about going home?"

"But Bethlehem is that way." She pointed with her finger.

"I know." He smiled. "I meant Nazareth."

THEY LIFTED JESUS ON THE DONKEY.

MARY

"Nazareth?" Her face lit up with joy. To be close to Ema and Abba again and her brothers and sisters. . .*home.*

Joseph nodded. "Nazareth is in Galilee. Herod's son Antipas rules there now, not Archelaus."

"And we'll be safe there?" Mary searched Joseph's face, looking for the fear she had read there yesterday.

"Yes." Joseph's face was calm and certain now. "We'll be safe in Nazareth. We can settle down at last."

Mary gave a skip of happiness. Then she glanced up again at Joseph. "You seem very sure about this. Have you been talking with a certain angel lately?"

He grinned. And she knew from the look of joy and peace in his eyes that Gabriel had visited her husband once again.

Her family was delighted to have them back in Nazareth, and they settled quickly into their old routines. Joseph went each day to his old carpentry shop, the same one where he had worked when Mary first met

JOSEPH WENT TO HIS OLD CARPENTRY SHOP.

MARY

him, and Mary busied herself each day with caring for her family. As Jesus grew older, He delighted them more and more. Everyone who knew Him loved Him. Even those who knew nothing of the wonder and mystery of His birth could tell that there was something unusual about Him, something joyful and loving that drew people to Him.

As Mary watched Jesus grow, she never forgot all the strange things that had happened during His early years, but she was glad that life was calmer now. As the years went by, each one so much like the one before, she wondered sometimes what God had in store for her Son. Just as quickly, she put the thought out of her mind. Wasn't it enough that Jesus was happy and healthy and safe? Would God ask anything more? With a little flicker of fear, she realized she almost wished that her Child was like any other child, with no enormous destiny waiting in His future.

When Jesus was twelve years old, Mary and Joseph took Him to Jerusalem for the Passover festival, just as they had every year since they had

THEY TOOK JESUS TO THE PASSOVER FESTIVAL.

MARY

returned to Nazareth. As always, Mary enjoyed the chance to be with friends and family who lived outside of Nazareth. She and Elizabeth were particularly glad to see one another, for they had remained close down through the years, even though they'd had few chances to be together. No other woman understood Mary's heart as much as Elizabeth did, and each year she looked forward to the chance to sit and talk with her.

When the festival was over, the band of travelers from Nazareth started home. Mary rode their donkey, enjoying the chance to talk with her mother and sisters as they traveled. She could see Joseph ahead of them, talking with the other men, and she assumed that Jesus was with the troop of children that ran along beside them, laughing and playing games as they went.

When they stopped for their evening meal, the crowd of people setting up camp was so thick that Mary could not see either her Son or her husband. She began to help prepare the supper, knowing that her family was bound to turn up soon, and she was

MARY RODE THE DONKEY.

MARY

not surprised when she felt Joseph's hand on her waist.

"There you are." He smiled down at her. "I knew if I found the cooking fire, I'd be bound to find you, too. Where's Jesus?"

Mary skewered some fresh meat and bent to lay the stick across the embers. "He must be with His friends somewhere. I haven't seen Him since this morning."

She stood up straight and searched the crowd of people milling around, feeling her first flicker of uneasiness. Jesus was more independent now that He was older, but she was very close to her Son, and He usually talked to her often throughout the day.

Joseph wiped a smudge of charcoal off her cheek and smiled. "Don't worry. I'll find Him. There's a group of kids playing some sort of game up on the hill. He's probably with them."

But He wasn't. And He wasn't with His grandfather or His uncles. He wasn't with any of their friends. Mary and Joseph had asked everyone if they had seen Him; no one had. At last, her stomach sick

SHE SEARCHED THE CROWD OF PEOPLE.

MARY

with fear, Mary met Joseph's eyes. "Where can He be?" she cried.

Joseph was already packing up their donkey. "Come on," he said. "We'll go back to Jerusalem. Somehow He must have been left behind."

"WE'LL GO BACK TO JERUSALEM."

WHAT WOULD A CHILD DO IN THE TEMPLE?

9

Three days later, they finally found Him. He was in the temple, sitting in the middle of a group of rabbis, deep in conversation. A small crowd had gathered around them to listen. Jesus didn't even look up when His parents joined the circle of people.

Mary's heart pounded with relief as she looked at her Son. He was safe after all. The last three days had been a nightmare as they searched everywhere they had been during the festival. They had never thought till now to look in the temple. After all, what would a child do in the temple?

What *was* He doing here? Mary edged closer

MARY

through the people. "Please let me through," she said desperately, anxious to touch Jesus, longing to know for sure He was really safe. Where had He been sleeping these last three nights? What had He eaten?

"Shh!" the person next to her said. "I want to hear the boy's answer to that last question."

Mary tried to listen, too, but she was too upset to understand her Son's words. She saw only that He looked happy and calm; He had obviously not been missing His mother and father.

After a moment, the man beside her turned to her. "Can you believe that a youngster like that would have such wisdom?" He shook his head. "How could a boy know such things? They say His name is Jesus of Nazareth."

"Yes," Mary said impatiently. "I know. He's my Son." At last she managed to push through the crowd, and she grabbed Jesus by the arm.

"What were You thinking of?" she asked Him, her voice shrill with fear and relief. "Why would You scare us like this? Your father and I have been frantic, searching for You everywhere."

"HE'S MY SON."

MARY

He looked up at her, surprised. "But why did you need to search?" He asked her. "You should have known that I would be in My Father's house."

"What are You talking about? Your father's house? Your father's house is back in Nazareth—which is where You would be right now if You had been where You were supposed to be."

Jesus didn't answer; He only looked into His mother's eyes. Mary drew in a deep breath. *He knows,* she realized. *He knows who He is.*

Their journey home to Nazareth was a quiet one. Joseph had started to scold Jesus for worrying them, and then he had fallen silent. Over Jesus' head, Mary and Joseph exchanged looks, their expressions confused and troubled.

Their life had been ordinary and quiet for so many years that they had both stopped thinking much about the angel who had guided them so often years before. But now Mary thought of him again. She wondered if Gabriel had been seated in the temple, listening to her Son, learning from His words

HE KNOWS WHO HE IS.

MARY

along with the rabbis and the rest.

She would like to sit down with Gabriel and have a talk some day, she thought. Maybe he could explain to her what her Son's purpose on earth was to be. She smiled, picturing Gabriel and herself having a chat some afternoon, the way she and Ema so often did, and she tried to imagine what he would say to her.

He is not only your Son, Mary. He is God's Son, too.

She did not hear the words out loud, and she saw no vision as Joseph had those four times. But she was suddenly certain that these were the words the angel would say to her.

Mary shivered. She put her hand on their donkey's warm neck, and she watched Jesus as He walked beside Joseph. *He is still just a Child*, she comforted herself. What could God want with Him now?

As though He sensed her gaze, Jesus turned and smiled at her, His gaze as bright and loving as always. *He is God's Son, too.* The words echoed in her mind.

HE IS GOD'S SON, TOO.

MARY

Mary took a deep breath, and then she lifted her head and squared her shoulders. *Yes, Lord. I want whatever You say.*

As the years went by, Mary said yes to God again and again as she watched Jesus grow taller and wiser with each passing month. He never again frightened them the way He had the year He was twelve. He seemed to understand that He needed to balance His responsibility to them, His earthly parents, with His responsibility to His heavenly Father.

When He reached adulthood and still their lives continued as quiet and uneventful as ever, Joseph wondered out loud to Mary if this quiet, simple life was all that God had planned for their Son.

"After all," he said, "maybe this is enough. He is an excellent carpenter. He is kind and loving to everyone. That way He has of listening so carefully to each person who talks to Him—it comforts people somehow. Maybe that is what the Lord is saying to us—that a quiet, honest, loving life is as pleasing to Him as fame and power."

HE REACHED ADULTHOOD.

MARY

"Yes," Mary said, her brow wrinkled. She knew that through her Son she had a new vision of the God she had served all her life. Before, God had always seemed distant somehow, a powerful, loving image that she could only catch glimpses of far in the distance. But now, God lived with her. He smiled at her every morning and touched her face with His familiar hand, He laughed at her table and thanked her for her smallest service to Him, and His arms were strong and warm when she was sad or afraid.

And yet at the same time, He was her Son, and she would give her life to keep Him safe and whole and happy. She sighed, her heart shadowed with fear. Although she said nothing to Joseph, somehow she was sure that God had something more in store for Jesus, something beyond the quiet, simple life He had lived with them so far.

When Jesus was thirty years old, the family traveled to Bethany where Mary's cousin Elizabeth now lived. Zechariah had died a few years earlier, and Elizabeth had grown very feeble, but she and Mary

THE FAMILY TRAVELED TO BETHANY.

MARY

still loved to sit and talk just as they always had. Mary was looking forward to that part of their visit, but for some reason she was dreading seeing Elizabeth's son John again.

John had grown into a strange young man. All his life he had been blunt and outspoken, but now he had a wildness about him that made Mary uncomfortable. He practiced no trade, and he no longer lived with his mother. Instead, he spent most of his time alone in the wilderness, wandering around dressed in a rough camel-hair robe that he bound with a leather belt. Elizabeth had told her that he ate only what he could find from the land, mostly locusts and wild honey. The very thought had made Mary cringe, but Elizabeth seemed unconcerned by her son's odd behavior. Mary, however, was glad that her own Son lived such an ordinary, quiet life.

Recently, Mary and Joseph had heard that people had begun to seek John out in the wilderness, so that they could listen to him speak and be baptized by him in the Jordan River. He was said to be a fiery preacher, speaking out against corruption, both in

JOHN HAD GROWN INTO A STRANGE YOUNG MAN.

MARY

the government and in people's hearts, and rumors were traveling around the country that John might even be the Messiah, the Anointed One who would rescue Israel from its bondage to Rome.

Joseph was eager to hear John preach, but Jesus had not commented on His cousin's ministry. Mary knew that He had heard the gossip, but He said nothing. He continued to help Joseph in the carpentry shop, just as He always had, and yet somehow the rumors about John made Mary uneasy. Something was changing, she sensed, and on the journey to Bethany she stayed close to Jesus, comforted by the peace she always felt in His presence.

As they neared Bethany, they noticed a large crowd gathered along the Jordan River, and they heard a man's voice shouting. Joseph lifted his head. "That's John! Let's go hear him."

Mary hung back. "Can't we go to Elizabeth's house first? She's expecting us, and I am tired."

Jesus took His mother's hand. "Come, Ema," He said quietly.

She looked up at Him and met His gaze. As

A LARGE CROWD GATHERED.

MARY

always, she saw the love and gentleness in His eyes, but she also saw a glimpse of the same strength and resolution she had first seen in Him in the temple when He was twelve. He smiled. "Will you come, Ema?"

She signed. "Yes. I will come with You."

As they drew nearer, she caught sight of John's wild curls rising above the heads of the crowd, and she knew he must be standing on something, a great stone maybe, or an upturned boat beside the river bank. His dark eyes flashed, and his words made her shiver.

"You brood of snakes!" he shouted. "Prove by the way you live that you have really turned from your sins and turned to God. Don't just say, 'We're safe—we're the descendants of Abraham.' That proves nothing. God can change these stones here into children of Abraham."

He waved his hand, and as the crowd parted a little, Mary saw that he was standing on a heap of tumbled river stone. Mary looked at the round, gray stones, and she thought suddenly of another stone, a

HE WAVED HIS HAND.

MARY

small round pebble that had dropped straight through Gabriel's hand.

She shivered again, but this time with a sense of joy and awe. God *could* do anything, and as she looked at John's wild, strong face, she knew he was not speaking poetically: John believed without a doubt in his mind that if God wanted, He could turn those ordinary stones into people, His people.

Lately, when Mary thought of God's great mansion, she imagined herself living in some small, quiet room, filled with sunlight and the ordinary smell of bread baking. She did not like to picture all the other strange rooms in the Lord's huge dwelling-place. Instead, she was content with the safe little corner He had given her, and she prayed that He would let her live out her days there, worshiping Him peacefully and quietly.

But now, something in John's words made her remember how great her Lord was and how immense was His mansion. She sensed in John a burning joy, and she knew he would stride fearlessly from room to room of God's home, wherever the Lord's Spirit led

SHE SENSED IN JOHN A BURNING JOY.

MARY

him. *Help me to have courage, Lord*, Mary whispered in her heart. *Help me to say yes to wherever You lead me.*

As though He had read her thoughts, Jesus stepped closer to her and brushed a kiss against her forehead. She looked up at Him, but He only smiled and turned back to listen to His cousin.

"Even now," John was saying, "the ax of God's judgment is poised, ready to sever your roots. Yes, every tree that does not produce good fruit will be chopped down and thrown into the fire."

Someone in the crowd shouted out to him, "What should we do?"

John turned toward the voice, his eyes glowing. "If you have two coats, give one to the poor. If you have food, share it with those who are hungry."

"How simple," Joseph said to Mary. "And yet how different our world would be if we all followed his direction."

There was a stir in the crowd, and a group of men pressed forward toward John. Joseph bent his head and whispered in Mary's ear, "Do you recognize

"WHAT SHOULD WE DO?"

MARY

those men? They're priests and Levites from the temple in Jerusalem." He looked grim. "I'm afraid John may find himself in trouble one of these days."

"Do you claim to be the Messiah?" one of the men asked John.

John turned to look at the man, his expression unreadable. "I am not the Messiah," he said flatly.

"Well then, who are you?" someone in the crowd shouted. "Are you Elijah?"

"No," John answered.

"Are you the Prophet?"

John grinned. "No, I am not."

"Then who are you?" asked one of the men from the temple. "Tell us, so we can give an answer to those who sent us. What do you have to say about yourself?"

John hesitated, his face thoughtful, and then he lifted his head and said clearly, "I am a voice shouting in the wilderness, 'Prepare a straight pathway for the Lord's coming!'"

Mary recognized his words as ones that the prophet Isaiah had spoken hundreds of years earlier,

"I AM A VOICE SHOUTING IN THE WILDERNESS!"

MARY

and the certainty and strength in John's voice made goose bumps creep across her skin. She looked up at Jesus, looking for some sort of reassurance, but His eyes were on His cousin. His face was as calm as ever, but she sensed that He was waiting for something.

"If you aren't the Messiah or Elijah or the Prophet," said one of the men from the temple, "what right do you have to baptize people the way you do?"

John shrugged his wide shoulders. "I baptize with water, but right here in the crowd is Someone you do not know, who will soon begin His ministry. I am not even worthy to be His slave." He looked over the heads of the people, directly at his cousin Jesus. "I baptize you with water, but He will baptize you with the Holy Spirit."

That night they sat late around Elizabeth's table, talking about the amazing way John spoke to people's hearts. Mary saw that Elizabeth was proud of her son, but Mary couldn't keep herself from asking her cousin as they cleared away the dishes, "Don't

"HE WILL BAPTIZE YOU WITH THE HOLY SPIRIT."

MARY

you worry what will happen to him? The Pharisees and the other temple officials will not be happy with what he is saying. They will be bound to make trouble for him."

Elizabeth only smiled. "He must follow his calling. I knew that from the moment he was conceived." Her faded eyes went to Jesus where He sat beside the fire with Joseph. "My son is like the person who lays a foundation," Elizabeth said softly. "It is your Son who will build the house."

Mary looked at Jesus for a long moment, and then she drew in a deep breath. She went to Him and knelt beside Him on the floor, looking up into His face. "Is it true then?" she asked softly. "Are you about to begin something new? Some ministry that will show others who You are?"

He smiled at her. "I must do what God tells me."

"What will You do?" Joseph asked Him quietly.

Jesus looked at His two earthly parents, His love for them clear in His gaze. He shrugged. "Well, to start with, I will ask John to baptize Me."

"I WILL ASK JOHN TO BAPTIZE ME."

JOHN BAPTIZED HIM.

10

Mary was not there to see when her Son was baptized, but she heard the story later from Elizabeth, who had heard it from her son.

At first, John had been reluctant to do what his cousin asked. "I am the one who needs to be baptized by You," he said, "so why are You coming to me?"

But Jesus answered him, "It must be done, because we must do everything that is right." So then John baptized Him.

"Afterward," Elizabeth told Mary, "as Jesus came up out of the water, an amazing thing happened. John says it looked as though a door opened

MARY

into heaven—and a dove fluttered out and flew straight to Jesus. It settled on His shoulder, and John heard a voice speak from heaven. The voice said, 'You are My beloved Son, and I am fully pleased with You.' "

As Mary listened to Elizabeth, she knew that their quiet, ordinary life was over now. She drew a deep breath and squared her shoulders. *Yes*, she told God. *Do whatever You want in our lives.*

Immediately, after His baptism, Jesus left home for over a month.

"Where is He?" their neighbors asked Mary and Joseph. "Where has He gone?"

"He went to be alone in the wilderness," Joseph told them quietly. But when he and Mary were alone, he asked her, "Will He be like John now, do you think? Living alone in the wilderness, dressing oddly, eating insects?"

Mary shook her head. "I do not know."

But after forty days, Jesus came home. He looked tired and thin, and Mary could see clearly that strong,

A DOVE FLEW STRAIGHT TO JESUS.

MARY

resolute part of Him that she had only glimpsed before. And yet His love and gentleness still lit His face the same as always. She hurried to cook Him a good meal, a little shy of this thin Man whose eyes burned in His sun-browned face.

But then He laughed and hugged her, and He was her own Jesus again. "That smells wonderful," He said as she dropped pieces of lamb into the hot oil.

"You must be hungry." She looked at Him over her shoulder. "Weren't You lonely out there all those days?"

He shook His head. "I wasn't alone."

She wiped her hands and turned to face Him. "Who was with You?"

"The animals." He smiled. "And the angels."

After that Jesus was seldom home. He had a group of friends who traveled with Him, and Mary was glad He was not alone as He had been while He was in the wilderness, but she missed her Son. Her heart was heavy with sorrow and fear, for she was certain that nothing would ever be the same again.

JESUS WAS SELDOM HOME.

MARY

The old days of quiet closeness with her Son were over forever. He belonged to others now, and she would never be close to Him again. And she feared for Him, uneasy now that she could no longer feed Him and care for Him, making certain He was safe and well.

During the time that Jesus was away, Joseph became sick and died, breaking Mary's heart. Of course Jesus came home for His father's funeral, but He brought His disciples with Him, and Mary had no chance to be alone with Him. She felt sick with grief and resentment as she watched Him leave her home. "Why should I say yes to You, Lord," she muttered, "when You have taken both my husband and my Son from me no matter what I say?" She bit her lip, ashamed of her anger at God, wishing she could talk to Joseph or Jesus about her feelings. But they were both gone, and she was alone.

The days were long and heavy for Mary. But she was looking forward to the wedding of Jacob and Rachel, Jesus' childhood friends, for she knew that Jesus was sure to be there. Maybe she would even

JOSEPH BECAME SICK AND DIED.

MARY

have a chance to spend some time with her Son.

At the wedding, Mary was glad to forget her sadness as she celebrated with Jacob and Rachel and their families and friends. Halfway through the party, though, she saw Jacob's father frown as he leaned close to his wife and said something in her ear.

"Oh no!" Jacob's mother looked around helplessly.

"What is it?" Mary asked her softly.

She hesitated, then whispered, "We've run out of wine." Her forehead puckered. "I knew we should have bought more, but. . . ." She shrugged, tears in her eyes.

Mary touched her arm gently. She understood how expensive a wedding feast could be, especially for a family who had little extra money. Her heart ached for the bridegroom and his family, for the guests would not be happy when they discovered that the wine was gone.

Automatically, as she always had when her heart was troubled, she sought out Jesus. "They have no more wine," she told Him quietly.

"THEY HAVE RUN OUT OF WINE."

MARY

He looked at her with understanding in His eyes, but His words were brusque. "How does that concern you and Me? My time has not yet come."

Mary looked at Him for a moment, surprised. She had not thought that He would necessarily solve the problem; she had merely wanted to tell Him what was wrong, for she had known that He would somehow make things better, just as He always did.

Over the years she had grown accustomed to sharing all her problems with Jesus, but since He had left home, she had begun again to deal with her troubles on her own. That was why her heart was so heavy lately, she realized. She had felt so alone, but she didn't have to, she saw. The time had come for others to share the great gift God had given her—but she could still tell her troubles to Jesus, just as she always had.

"I have missed You, Son," she told Him.

He smiled. "Look in your heart, Ema. I am with you always, forever."

Tears sprang to Mary's eyes, but she squared her shoulders and lifted her head high. As clearly as if a

"I AM WITH YOU ALWAYS, FOREVER."

MARY

voice spoke to her out loud, she knew what she should do next. She turned to the servants who stood nearby. "Do whatever He tells you," she told them. She laughed to herself. "Say yes to whatever He says."

Jesus gave her a small smile. "It *is* My time, isn't it?" His eyes traveled around the courtyard, and then He pointed to the line of six stone waterpots that stood along the edge of the wall. "Fill the jars with water," He told the servants.

The servants muttered to each other, their eyebrows raised. They looked from Jesus to His mother, and something they saw in their faces must have convinced them. Without another word, they filled the jars to the brim.

"What is He doing?" a friend whispered to her, but Mary only shook her head. She watched her Son, waiting to see what He would do next. She had learned long ago that when she brought a problem to Him, she needed to simply wait for Him to act in His own time and in His own way. If she came with a solution already in her mind, she was

"FILL THE JARS WITH WATER."

usually disappointed—but in the end, she always realized that He had known best all along.

Jesus leaned over the jars of water. He made no movement, spoke no word, but simply looked down into the clear water. He turned back to the servants. "Please," He said, "dip some out and take it to the master of ceremonies."

Mary watched as the master of ceremonies tasted from the cup. The man's eyes lit, and he motioned to the bridegroom to come to him. "Usually a host serves the best wine first," he said loudly. "Then, when everyone is full and doesn't care, he brings out the less expensive wines. But you have kept the best until now!" He clapped the groom on the back and laughed out loud, then took another deep drink of the wine.

After the wedding, to Mary's delight, Jesus spent a few days with His family. This time she did not mind that He brought His disciples with Him. They were good men, and she found herself laughing at Peter's jokes and enjoying John's quiet understanding. But

THE MASTER OF CEREMONIES TASTED FROM THE CUP.

MARY

she was grateful one night when Jesus joined her on the roof, and they sat together alone in the darkness, looking up at the stars as they had done so many times when Jesus was a child.

After a moment she broke the silence. "This is Your time now, isn't it, Son?"

"Yes." He tipped His head back against the stone wall and stretched out His long legs. "I must get busy now with My heavenly Father's business." He turned toward her, and she felt His eyes search her face in the darkness. "But I am sorry if it pains you, Ema."

She shook her head. "You are the Messiah, Son. I always knew that. Your earthly father would be proud of You. As I am."

She saw the flash of His white teeth. "People expect the Messiah to liberate Israel from Rome. Is that what you expect, Ema?"

For a long moment she gazed up at the bright stars, wondering what it was that she expected. She had feared the future for a long time, she realized, ever since Jesus was a baby, as though the future held

"YOU ARE THE MESSIAH, SON."

MARY

some dark, horrible secret that would be too terrible for her to face. She remembered again the third astrologer's strange gift of myrrh, and she shuddered. And then she thought of Gabriel's bright face, and the calm, certain joy she had seen in his eyes. She sighed.

"I have learned, Son, that You and Your Father seldom do things the way I expect. I think my ways would be better—but in the end, Your ways are far better than anything I could ever imagine. So I might as well say yes from the very beginning—and then just wait and see what miracle You will do."

"Like you did at the wedding."

She smiled and nodded. "Yes." She looked at Him through the darkness. "Why did You do it? Why did You turn the water into wine? Such a little thing for You to bother with, such a small way for You to reveal Yourself."

Again she saw the gleam of His white teeth in the darkness. "Little things are important to My Father."

He reached for her hand. "The future will not be easy for you, Ema. But do not stop saying yes."

"LITTLE THINGS ARE IMPORTANT TO MY FATHER."

MARY STOOD AT THE FOOT OF A CROSS.

11

"No!"

Three years later, Mary stood at the foot of a cross on Skull Hill, gazing up at her Son. Around her people laughed and jeered and shouted insults. "No," she cried again, longing to silence them. She tipped her face up toward the strange purple sky. "You cannot let this happen, Lord. He is Your *Son*. How can You turn Your face and let Him die this way?" Her words dissolved into tears; she turned her head into her sister's shoulder.

The days that had led up to this afternoon had been like a nightmare. Joseph had been right to fear

MARY

the government all those years ago when Jesus was just a baby, for in the end it was the government that had sentenced Jesus to death. Jewish religious leaders had done their part, though. They had formed a trap that had closed tighter and tighter around Jesus, until at last it shut tight on Him. But until the last moment, she had believed that He would somehow work a miracle and turn things around. She had not believed He would end up here, dying on a cross with two criminals.

Her sister held her close, but her arms were shaking. Beyond her, Mary caught a glimpse of the stricken faces of Mary Magdalene and Salome. And then she felt a gentle hand on her shoulder. She turned and looked into John's face.

"He wants to speak to you." His face was drawn, but his brown eyes were steady and full of compassion. "Come."

Mary pulled away from her sister and moved closer to the cross. She could hardly bear to see the nails that pierced her Son's skin; she longed to wipe the blood from His face and mend His wounds. But

HER SISTER HELD HER CLOSE.

MARY

she could do nothing. *How can You do this, God? If I had the power, I would take Him home and heal Him; I would rescue Him and keep Him safe forever. I have no power to do that—but You do. How can You allow this to happen? He is Your Son, too. Don't You love Him, as I do? Aren't You a God of love? I don't understand.*

She swallowed back her tears and tipped her face up toward Jesus. "Son." Her voice quavered, but she hoped He would hear all her love in that one word.

"Ema." The familiar syllables brought fresh tears to her eyes. Through the watery blur, she saw that His face was tight with pain, but His eyes were filled with the same quiet love she had always seen there. She reached out to Him, longing to touch Him.

"Let John be your son now, Ema," He said. His gaze moved to John. "She will be your mother now."

John put his arm around Mary's shoulders. "Yes, Lord. Do not worry for Your mother. I will take care of her. And I will love her as my own mother."

Mary gazed up at her Son, trying to understand why this horrible thing was happening. He had the

"LET JOHN BE YOUR SON NOW."

MARY

power to get down from the cross all by Himself, she knew, for she had seen the miracles He could do. She thought of His friend Lazarus, whom He had raised from the dead. And then there had been the little girl, and Peter's mother. Each of these people He had saved from death's dark hold. And yet He was allowing Himself to be killed; He was saying yes to a criminal's death. "Why?" she whispered. "Why?"

But He did not hear her, or if He did, He gave her no answer. "I am thirsty," she heard Him say.

She longed to get Him a cup of cold water; she remembered all the nights when He was small, when she or Joseph had gotten up to bring their Son a drink. Now, she could do nothing for Him. Dazed, she watched as someone soaked a sponge with sour wine, then stuck it on the end of a long branch and lifted it so Jesus could suck the moisture from it. He tasted it, then threw back His head.

"It is finished!" His head slumped forward. Her Son was dead.

The rest of that long day was a blur for Mary. The

HER SON WAS DEAD.

MARY

crowd that had gathered slowly dispersed, but she and John and the other women stayed, watching that motionless body hanging from the cross. Soldiers came and broke the legs of the other two men who were being killed with Jesus, and Mary was oddly relieved when the soldiers left her Son's quiet body alone. She flinched, though, when one of them thrust his sword into Jesus' side.

Finally, John led her gently away and brought her to his house. He gave her something to eat, but she only sat at the table, not eating, not thinking, staring dully at a small beetle that was crawling along the edge of the tabletop. Suddenly, she jumped up.

"His body! What will happen to Him now? We must go get Him. Where will we bury Him?"

John shook his head and pushed her gently back into her chair. "Joseph of Arimathea has gotten permission from Pilate to take Jesus away. Joseph has a new tomb where he will bury Him. And Nicodemus has brought myrrh and aloe to embalm Him—and a long piece of linen to wrap Him in."

Mary's mouth twisted. "Myrrh," she said bitterly.

THE SOLDIERS LEFT HER SON'S BODY ALONE.

MARY

"I hate myrrh."

John shrugged his shoulders helplessly. "I wish I knew how to comfort you."

Mary looked up at him and saw the tears that slid down his own cheeks. She shook her head. "No one can comfort us now. Jesus is dead." The words made her gasp with fresh pain.

"Yes." John's voice was heavy with sorrow. "But Jesus promised us that He would send us the Holy Spirit to comfort us. Remember what He said?"

Mary shook her head, barely listening to John's words, too overwhelmed with her pain.

John looked off into space, remembering. "This is what He said, Mary. Listen:

" *'If you love Me, obey My commandments. And I will ask the Father, and He will give you another Comforter, who will never leave you. He is the Holy Spirit, who leads into all truth. The world at large cannot receive Him, because it isn't looking for Him and doesn't recognize Him. But*

TEARS SLID DOWN HIS CHEEKS.

MARY

you do, because He lives with you now and later will be in you. No, I will not abandon you as orphans—I will come to you. In just a little while the world will not see Me again, but you will. For I will live again, and you will too.'"

Mary shook her head. "How can He live again? I don't understand what He meant. We don't know how to work the miracles He did for Lazarus and Peter's mother."

John sighed. "No. We don't." He took her hand. "Come. I have a bed prepared for you. Try to get some rest."

Mary lay in bed staring into the darkness hour after hour. She felt as though someone had stabbed her through the heart, and she remembered the old man's prophecy so many years ago: *A sword will pierce your very soul.* Well, Simeon had been right about that. But why? Why had God sent His Son only to allow Him to be killed?

A SWORD WILL PIERCE YOUR VERY SOUL.

MARY

"No," she muttered. "I will not say yes to You this time, Lord. Whatever I say will make no difference. Jesus will still be dead. But I will not say yes to my Son's death."

At last she fell into a fitful sleep, but her dreams were troubled and dark. Toward morning she woke up and lay staring at the window, a light gray square against the darker wall.

But it will *make a difference.*

She had fallen asleep again, she realized, but this time she felt a sense of peace steal into her heart. And the voice she heard speaking in her dream was Jesus'.

"What will make a difference?" she asked Him.

In the dream, He sat down cross-legged beside her sleeping mat and smiled down at her. *You know what I mean, Ema. It will make a difference whether you say yes or no to My death. It will make a difference in your own heart and in your own life. God can turn even the darkest, most horrible thing into something amazing and glorious, something far better than anything you could ever imagine. But first*

THE VOICE SHE HEARD IN HER DREAM WAS JESUS'.

MARY

you have to say yes.

"Not this time," she told Him. "I can't say yes to You being dead. And I could never see anything good in Your death. Never."

Yes, Ema. You can.

"No. This is the worst thing that ever happened to me. It is the worst thing that ever happened in the entire world, ever. Worse than when our people suffered in slavery in Egypt, worse even than when our father and mother, Adam and Eve, first sinned in the Garden. You are the Son of God. And they killed You." Mary choked on the words.

Yes. And it is the worst thing that ever happened. But it is also the best thing. It is the reason that I came.

In her dream, Mary frowned. "How can that be?"

Don't you remember what I said? God loved the world so much that He sent Me, His only Son, so that everyone who believes in Me will never die, but will live forever.

He had said that, Mary remembered now. "But why did You have to die? Couldn't You have saved

"THEY KILLED YOU."

MARY

the world without dying?"

He shook his head. *No. I had to give everything.* He smiled and touched her face. *Don't be sad, Ema. I am leaving you with a gift of peace—peace of mind and heart. And the peace I give isn't like the peace the world gives. So don't be troubled or afraid. Remember what I told you: I am going away, but I will come back to you again. If you really love Me, you will be very happy for Me, because now I can go to the Father, who is greater than I am.*

He took her hand in His. *Say yes, Ema,* He whispered, and then He was gone.

Mary opened her eyes. She didn't think she had dreamed a vision, as Joseph used to so long ago when the angel had spoken to him in his sleep. No, hers had been an ordinary dream—but she remembered now that during the days before His death, Jesus had really spoken the same words that He had in her dream. She just hadn't understood then.

The window was now a bright square of blue sky, and sunlight flickered across the earth floor beside her bed. Tears still leaked out of her eyes, but

HE TOOK HER HAND IN HIS.

MARY

she drew in a deep breath and whispered, "Yes." And then she sat up and said it more loudly, "Yes! I am the Lord's servant, and I am willing to accept whatever He wants."

Mary was just as sad the next day, but despite her sadness, she continued to say yes to God in her heart. She and John talked quietly, remembering things Jesus had said. When she went to bed that night, she fell asleep at once and slept without any dreams.

In the morning she got up and began preparing food for the day. As she busied herself with ordinary household tasks, she sang psalms, despite her heavy heart. And then as she and John sat down to their morning meal, Mary Magdalene burst into the house. She stood panting, her face troubled and confused.

"What is it?" John asked in surprise.

When Mary Magdalene had caught her breath enough to speak, she gasped, "They have taken the Lord's body out of the tomb, and I don't know where they have put Him!"

"THEY HAVE TAKEN THE LORD'S BODY OUT OF THE TOMB!"

THEY FOUND AN EMPTY TOMB.

12

About three months later, Mary knelt with a group of Jesus' believers, praying together as they did every day now. As they prayed, Mary thought back over all that had happened since that dark afternoon when Jesus had died.

Her Son had risen from the dead! She could still barely grasp the miracle that had happened. They had lain Him in a grave, but death could not keep Jesus. When John had gone with Peter to see if what Mary Magdalene had said was true, they found an empty tomb. The linen cloths that had wrapped Jesus' body were neatly folded and lying

MARY

on the stone shelf, and their hearts had been filled with a wild impossible joy. Jesus had conquered death forever.

After that, first Mary Magdalene had seen Jesus, and then He had come to His disciples. In the end, about five hundred people had seen Him, including His mother.

Mary remembered how wonderful it had been to be with her Son again. Sometimes His death had seemed like a bad dream that she could forget all about. But she knew that His death was no dream. Because Jesus had loved the world enough to die, everyone who believed in Jesus would one day live with Him for eternity.

She had longed to keep Him with her, to go back to the old days when He was only her Son, not the world's Messiah. But He had warned her that He could not stay with her. "Don't cling to Me," He had told her. "Soon I must ascend to the Father."

She hadn't understood what He meant—but by then she knew that Jesus might do anything at all. She couldn't predict His behavior. She certainly

JESUS HAD COME TO HIS DISCIPLES.

MARY

couldn't control Him. All she could do was nod her head. "Yes, Lord," she murmured, and His smile was her reward.

But many of the disciples still hoped that Jesus would free Israel from Rome after all. They kept asking Him, "Now will You restore our kingdom to us?"

Each time they asked the question, Jesus merely shook His head. "The Father will decide when your earthly freedom will come," He told them patiently. "He is the One who sets those dates, and they are not for you to know. But when the Holy Spirit has come upon you, you will receive power and will tell people about Me everywhere—in Jerusalem, throughout Judea, in Samaria, and to the ends of the earth."

Soon after that, one day when they were all talking with Jesus up on the Mount of Olives outside Jerusalem, He was suddenly taken up into the sky. As they watched, He disappeared into a cloud. Mary strained her eyes to catch one last glimpse of Him, her heart overwhelmed with joy and sorrow and wonder. And then some change in the light made her turn around.

HE WAS SUDDENLY TAKEN UP INTO THE SKY.

MARY

Two white-robed men stood there among them, their skin glowing like gold. "Gabriel!" she cried.

He smiled at her, and then he turned to the apostles. "Men of Galilee," he said to them, "why are you standing here staring at the sky? Jesus has been taken away from you into heaven. And someday, just as you saw Him go, He will return."

After that, all of Jesus' followers had begun meeting together every day in the upstairs room of the house where many of them were staying. Some of them thought they were waiting for Jesus' return, as the angel had promised, but Mary had a feeling that they were waiting for something else, something she could not imagine. After all, her Son never did things exactly the way she expected. He always took her by surprise.

Now, as they knelt together praying, she suddenly had a feeling that the thing for which they were waiting was about to happen. She raised her head, listening.

At first, all she heard was a tiny whisper, like a breath of wind blowing through the open window.

THEY KNELT TOGETHER PRAYING.

MARY

John heard it, too, she saw; his eyes met hers, and she saw the same awe and delight there that filled her own heart. Soon the noise grew louder, until heaven roared with wind. The storm swept through the house.

Mary watched in wonder as flames of fire settled on each person in the room. She felt the burning heat on her own head and in her own heart.

This was the Holy Spirit, she realized, the Comforter whom Jesus had promised He would send. She could feel Him knocking on her heart's door, and she understood that by His power, God's great house would be built across the entire world, down through the ages. This was the kingdom her Son had come to build, not an earthly one as so many had hoped. As always, His plans were far greater than theirs.

And she would be a part of her Son's amazing kingdom, God's endless mansion of love. All she had to do was say that one familiar word. "Yes!" she cried and flung wide her heart's door. And the Holy Spirit came in and filled her with His power.

THIS WAS THE HOLY SPIRIT.

AWESOME BOOKS FOR KIDS!
The Young Reader's Christian Library
Action, Adventure, and Fun Reading!

This series for young readers ages 8 to 12 is action-packed, fast-paced, and Christ-centered! With exciting illustrations on every other page following the text, kids won't be able to put these books down! Over 100 illustrations per book. All books are paperbound. The unique size (4 $^1/_8$" x 5 $^3/_8$") makes these books easy to take anywhere!

A Great Selection to Satisfy All Kids!

Abraham Lincoln	Elijah	Miriam
Billy Graham	Esther	Moses
Billy Sunday	Florence	Paul
Christopher	Nightingale	Peter
Columbus	Hudson Taylor	The Pilgrim's
Clara Barton	In His Steps	Progress
Corrie ten Boom	Jesus	Roger Williams
Daniel	Jim Elliot	Ruth
David	Joseph	Samuel
David Brainerd	Little Women	Samuel Morris
David Livingstone	Luis Palau	Sojourner Truth
Deborah	Lydia	

Available wherever books are sold.
Or order from: Barbour Publishing, Inc., P.O. Box 719
Uhrichsville, Ohio 44683
http://www.barbourbooks.com

$2.50 each retail, plus $1.00 for postage and handling per order.
Prices subject to change without notice.